TO THE RESCUE

FIRE TRUCKS THEN AND NOW

TO THE RESCUE

FIRE TRUCKS THEN AND NOW

Steve Otfinoski

BENCHMARK BOOKS

MARSHALL CAVENDISH
NEW YORK

Benchmark Books
Marshall Cavendish Corporation
99 White Plains Road
Tarrytown, New York 10591-9001

Library of Congress-in-Publication Data
Otfinoski, Steven.
To the rescue : fire trucks then and now / by Steven Otfinoski.
    p.   cm. — (Here we go!)
Includes bibliographical references and index.
Summary: Examines the history of firefighting vehicles and describes
different kinds that are used today.
ISBN 0-7614-0406-6 (lib. bdg.)
1. Fire engines—Juvenile literature. [1. Fire engines.] I.Title II.Series:
Here we go! (New York, N.Y.)
TH9372.087   1997   628.9'25—dc20   96-18480   CIP   AC

Photo research by Matthew Dudley

Cover photo: *The Image Bank:* Grant V. Faint

The photographs in this book are used by permission and through the
courtesy of: *Hans Halberstadt/Arms Communications:* 1, 10, 12, 14, 15, 16,
17 (top and bottom), 26, 30, back cover. *The Image Bank:* Patti
McConville, 2, 19 (top), 22; Pamela Zilly, 6–7; Grant V. Faint, 18, 20; Ted
Kawalerski, 19 (bottom); Any Caulfield, 21; Marc Soloman, 23; GK and
Vicki Hart, 24; Alfredo Tessi, 28–29; Cliff Feulner, 32. *Corbis-Bettmann:* 7,
8 (top and bottom), 9, 11, 13 (top and bottom). *Photo Researchers, Inc.:*
Susan Kuklin, 24–25; Sam C. Pierson Jr., 25; Sandved Photography, 27.

Printed in the United States of America

6   5   4   3   2   1

To Matt,

the brave and adventurous firefighter in our family

ire!"
That familiar cry is heard
every day across America.
There are more than three hundred fires
every hour in the United States.
Fire trucks zoom firefighters to the rescue
to save lives and property.
But it wasn't always that way.

In colonial days there were no fire trucks.

People carried buckets of water by hand from the town well or the nearest pond or river.

This was called a bucket brigade.

Anyone who passed by and didn't lend a hand had a bucket of water dumped over their head!

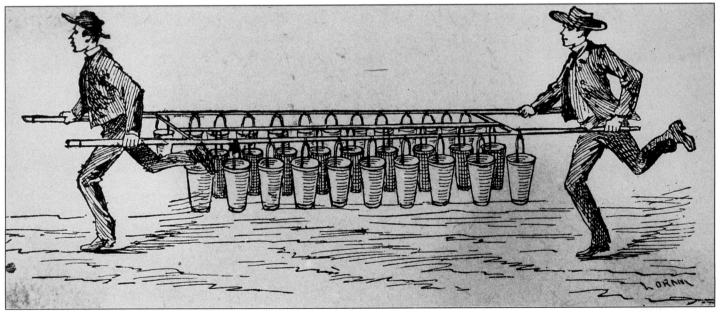

The first fire trucks had a pump that pushed
water out through a hose.
It took as many as twenty–eight men to work the pump.
The water came from a tank built in the truck.
People had to work quickly to keep the tank filled,
pouring in bucket after bucket of water.

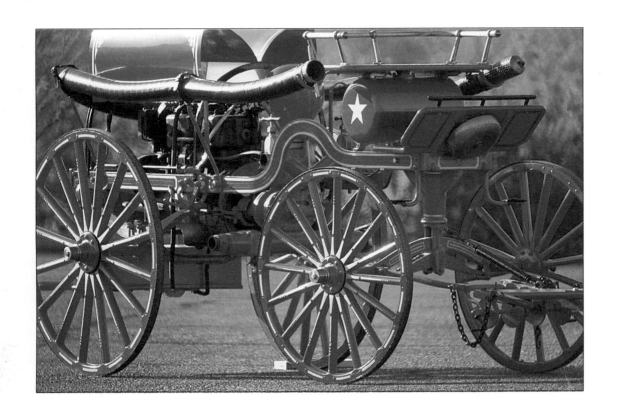

In 1852 two men in Cincinnati built the first steam–powered fire engine. They called the new engine Uncle Joe Ross after a local politician who supported their invention.

In a contest, Uncle Joe beat a hand pumper. But the steam engine needed only a few men to run it. Many firefighters were afraid they would lose their jobs. They said "no" to Uncle Joe and stuck stubbornly to their hand pumpers for years.

Both hand pumpers and steam engines were pulled by horses.

Other new equipment helped firefighters do a better job.
A mechanical water tower allowed them to spray water from a hose without having to climb a ladder.
Can you see how it worked from the picture (top right)?
Early hook and ladder trucks carried hooks to open windows and tear down burning walls.

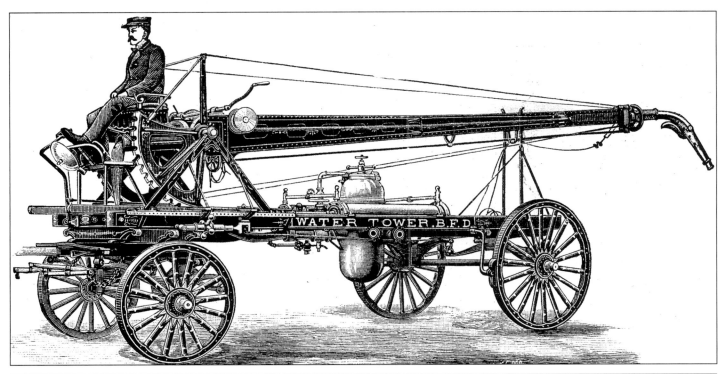

The first gasoline–powered fire trucks broke down a lot.
Many departments stayed with their horse–drawn trucks.
But in time, better trucks were built.
Fire trucks, like the one from 1930 below, rang a bell to warn
other vehicles to get out of the way.

Here are some classic fire trucks from the 1940s and 1950s.
These trucks could go faster than the earlier ones.
They carried better gear for fighting fires, too.

Today's firefighters are always ready for an alarm.
All their equipment has its proper place,
so the firefighters can get it quickly.
Fire trucks are fully outfitted and ready to roll.
Even the firehouse dog, a Dalmatian, is on the alert.
These dogs make good pets for the firefighters.

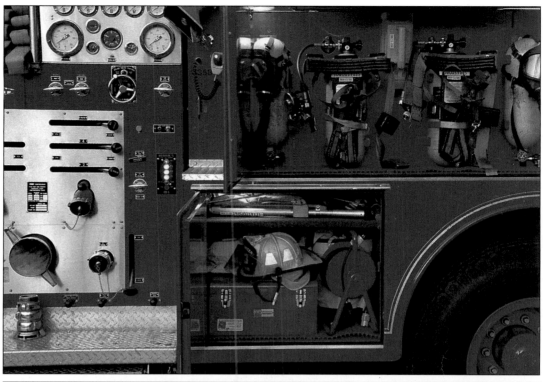

Once an alarm is called in, the firefighters stop whatever they're doing. They quickly put on their fire suits and climb aboard the trucks.

The fire trucks race to the scene of the fire, and the fire chief's car rushes right behind. The firefighters turn on their sirens and flashing lights. This tells other drivers to get out of the way—fast!

Three different trucks rush to the scene.
The pumper truck takes in water from fire hydrants.
The firefighters stretch hoses from the truck to the fire.
Then the truck pumps the water out through the hoses
at about 155 gallons of water per minute.

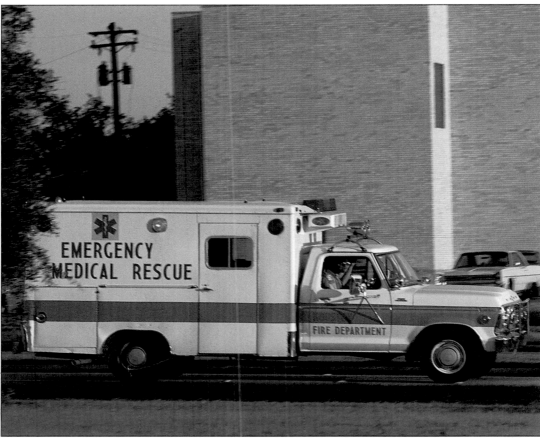

Ladder trucks allow firefighters to get near the fire.
From the top of the ladder, firefighters rescue people and pets.
Aerial ladders can reach up to the eighth story of a building.
A special gun hose can spray up to one thousand gallons of water
a minute.
Rescue trucks carry firefighting equipment and medical supplies.
They can also take injured people to the hospital.

Other special fire vehicles include this airport crash truck.
It fights fires on airplanes.
Water won't put out fires feeding on jet fuel and gasoline,
so the airport crash truck sprays foam or dry chemicals instead.
These smother the fire by cutting off its air supply.
Fire boats put out fires on ships and in waterfront buildings.
They can pump water right out of the sea.

Fire trucks have changed a lot over the years.
Many trucks are now lime green or yellow
instead of red.
These colors are easier for other drivers
to see at night.
But one thing hasn't changed.
Fire trucks still rush to the rescue!

INDEX

FIND OUT MORE

Gibbons, Gail. *Fire! Fire!* New York: HarperCollins, 1984.

Loeper, John J. *By Hook and Ladder: The Story of Fire Fighting in America.* New York: Atheneum, 1981.

Maas, Robert. *Fire Fighters.* New York: Scholastic, 1989.

Rockwell, Anne. *Fire Engines.* New York: Dutton, 1986.

STEVE OTFINOSKI has written more than sixty books for children. He also has a theater company called *History Alive!* that performs plays for schools about people and events from the past. Steve lives in Stratford, Connecticut, with his wife and two children.